BEARCUB BIOS

ACTOR AND CHILD ACTIVIST

by Rachel Rose

Consultant: Beth Gambro
Reading Specialist, Yorkville, Illinois

Minneapolis, Minnesota

Teaching Tips

BEFORE READING

- Look at the cover of the book. Discuss the picture and the title.
- Ask readers to brainstorm a list of what they already know about Jennifer Garner. What can they expect to see in this book?
- Go on a picture walk, looking through the pictures to discuss vocabulary and make predictions about the text.

DURING READING

- Read for purpose. Encourage readers to look for key pieces of information they can expect to see in biographies.
- Ask readers to look for the details of the book. What happened to Jennifer Garner at different times of her life?
- If readers encounter an unknown word, ask them to look at the sounds in the word. Then, ask them to look at the rest of the page. Are there any clues to help them understand?

AFTER READING

- Encourage readers to pick a buddy and reread the book together.
- Ask readers to name three things Jennifer Garner has done throughout her life. Go back and find the pages that tell about these things.
- Ask readers to write or draw something they learned about Jennifer Garner.

Credits:
Cover and title page, ©Lionel Hahn/Alamy, RealCG Animation Studio/Shutterstock; 3, ©Amy Sussman/Staff/Getty Images; 5, ©Chelsea Guglielmino/Staff/Getty Images; 7, ©Paul Smith/Alamy; 9, ©Joel Shawn/Shutterstock; 11, ©Chamberednautilus/Wikimedia; 13, ©Steve Granitz/Contributor/Getty Images; 15, ©Noam Galai/Stringer/Getty Images; 17, ©Paul Morigi/Contributor/Getty Images; 19, ©Richard B. Levine/Newscom; 21, ©Rich Fury/KCA2021/Contributor/Getty Images; 22, ©DFree/Shutterstock; 23, ©ViDI Studio/Shutterstock; 23, ©Tomasz Bidermann/Shutterstock; 23, ©Monkey Business Images/Shutterstock; 23, ©Kozlik/Shutterstock; 23, ©Jeff Vinnick/Contributor/Getty Images; 23, ©New Africa/Shutterstock

Library of Congress Cataloging-in-Publication Data

Names: Rose, Rachel, 1968- author.
Title: Jennifer Garner : actor and child activist / by Rachel Rose.
Description: Minneapolis, Minnesota : Bearport Publishing, [2023] | Series: Bearcub bios | Includes bibliographical references and index.
Identifiers: LCCN 2022002320 (print) | LCCN 2022002321 (ebook) | ISBN 9781636917177 (library binding) | ISBN 9781636917245 (paperback) | ISBN 9781636917313 (ebook)
Subjects: LCSH: Garner, Jennifer, 1972---Juvenile literature. | Motion
  picture actors and actresses--United States--Biography--Juvenile
  literature. | Television actors and actresses--United States--Biography--Juvenile literature. | Women political
  activists--United States--Biography--Juvenile literature.
Classification: LCC PN2287.G3855 R67 2023 (print) | LCC PN2287.G3855
  (ebook) | DDC 791.4302/8092 [B]--dc23/eng/20220208
LC record available at https://lccn.loc.gov/2022002320
LC ebook record available at https://lccn.loc.gov/2022002321

Copyright © 2023 Bearport Publishing Company. All rights reserved. No part of this publication may be reproduced in whole or in part, stored in any retrieval system, or transmitted in any form or by any means, electronic, mechanical, photocopying, recording, or otherwise, without written permission from the publisher.

For more information, write to Bearport Publishing, 5357 Penn Avenue South, Minneapolis, MN 55419. Printed in the United States of America.

Contents

Fan Favorite! 4

Jennifer's Life 6

Did You Know?............................ 22

Glossary 23

Index 24

Read More 24

Learn More Online......................... 24

About the Author 24

Fan Favorite!

Jennifer Garner smiled and waved.

Fans cheered her name.

They loved to see one of their favorite **actors**.

Jennifer's Life

Jennifer grew up in West Virginia.

She has always been close with her family.

Jennifer has two sisters.

One sister is older and one is younger.

As a child, Jennifer loved to dance.

She joined the marching band in high school.

Jennifer loved to **perform**.

When she was older, Jennifer went to **college**.

She took acting classes.

Then, Jennifer went to look for acting jobs.

Where Jennifer went to college

Jennifer got small **roles** on many TV shows.

After a few years, she got a big job.

She was the star in a show about a **spy**.

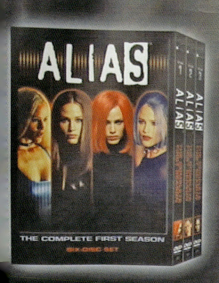

Soon, Jennifer was in movies.

But Jennifer wanted to do more than act.

She cared about helping children, too.

Jennifer wants all children to go to good schools.

She raises money to help them.

Sometimes, she visits kids in schools!

Jennifer also wants children to be healthy.

She started a **company** that makes food.

Jennifer even grows some of the food on her farm.

Jennifer is busy with her acting.

She works hard to help children.

Jennifer will keep working hard and doing what she loves!

Did You Know?

Born: April 17, 1972

Family: Patricia (mother), William (father), Susannah (sister), Melissa (sister)

When she was a kid: She danced for six hours a day.

Special fact: Jennifer's mom grew up on a farm. Jennifer now owns the farm!

Jennifer says: "A little kindness goes a long way."

Life Connections

Jennifer loves to act. She helps children, too. What do you love to do? Can some of those things help other people?

Glossary

actors people who act in movies and TV shows

college school that people can go to after high school

company a group or person that does a job

perform to act or dance for a group of people

roles parts played by actors

spy a person whose job is to find out secrets

Index

acting 10, 14, 20, 22
children 14, 16, 18, 20, 22
food 18
schools 8, 16
sisters 6–7, 22
TV shows 12
West Virginia 6

Read More

Ardely, Anthony. *I Can Be an Actor (I Can Be Anything!)*. New York: Gareth Stevens, 2019.

Bell, Samantha. *You Can Work in Movies (You Can Work in the Arts)*. North Mankato, MN: Capstone, 2019.

Learn More Online

1. Go to **www.factsurfer.com** or scan the QR code below.
2. Enter "**Jennifer Garner**" into the search box.
3. Click on the cover of this book to see a list of websites.

About the Author

Rachel Rose is a writer who lives in California. Her favorite books to write are about people who lead inspiring lives.